The Perfect Man for Me

A Short Story

Marriage/Temptation/Romance/Decisions

Library of Congress Control # 1-1292167631

ISBN – 13: 978-0615991160

ISBN – 10: 0615991165

Other Books by Stephanie Lahart

Teens Matter Most

Overcoming Life's Obstacles

Connect with Stephanie Lahart

twitter.com/1lahart

facebook.com/1lahartstephanie

pinterest.com/stephanielahart

about.me/stephanie.lahart

Contents

Chapter One

Welcome to my world. Well, my boring world that is. My husband and I will be celebrating our 25th anniversary in three more days. Excitement doesn't even enter my mind, and quite honestly, I've been feeling this way about my marriage for the past two years now. I thought I married the perfect man for me, but it's time for me to face the truth and be honest with myself.

For about a year now, I've been thinking about the perfect man for me. I've been thinking things that a wife shouldn't, but I can't seem to control myself. I wish I could make these thoughts go away, but the feelings that I have are much too strong.

These four men, one being my husband, each have something that I strongly desire. Yes, you heard me correctly, four men. They all have things that would make them the perfect man for me.

How rude of me! Before I get into all of the details about my life, let me tell you a little bit about myself first.

Back down memory lane.

My name is Hannah-Marie. I was born and raised in Clearwater, Florida in the spring of 1959. My mom and dad both adored me. I was their only child and everybody knew that I was their pride and joy.

They owned a small neighborhood store where they sold ice cream, freshly baked goods, sandwiches, and drinks. Everybody in the neighborhood loved my parents. They were devotedly in love with one another and they both took pride in making other people smile and giving great service to their customers. They were well respected by everybody. Nobody had an ill word to say about them. My mom and dad were both lovely people inside and out.

We were a small family of three, but the bond that we shared was genuine and rare. They were the hands-on type of parents. You name it, we did it: board games, skating, bike riding, hiking, cooking together, family walks, going to the beach, camping, etc. They were a joy to be around.

This joy, this genuine happiness, because of one moment, was robbed from me. When I was thirteen years old, my mom and dad had went out one night to a friend's birthday party. My uncle Ralph, my dad's brother, drove down to watch me while they were at the party. On the way home, three blocks away from where we lived, they were killed by a drunk driver. My life was shattered. I lost the two people that gave me life. I lost the two people that loved me the most.

After my mom and dad's death, I went to live with my uncle Ralph, his wife, and four children. The first two years were extremely difficult and painful for me. Living with my uncle kept the death of my parents fresh in my mind, especially my dad. They looked just alike, except my dad was about three inches taller than my uncle was. I struggled in school and I pretty much kept to myself. I went from being outgoing and fun to be around, to quiet and withdrawn. I felt hopeless, lost, and confused.

Through it all, my uncle and his wife treated me just like I was their own child. They made me feel right at home. I never felt like I didn't belong there. They had ample space in their home, so I had my own bed, but I shared a room with my youngest cousin Elizabeth. She was such a sweet person and her smile brightened any room. My other three cousins were a bit older than we were and they were really cool as well. Unlike some families, they all got along very well with one another. I guess it runs in the family.

I lived at my uncle's house for seven years. When I turned twenty, I felt it was time for me to live on my own and start my life as a responsible adult. They didn't want me to leave, but I needed to do it for myself. I wanted to explore more, experience more, and meet new people. It was important for me to get out there and make something of myself. I will always be grateful to all of them, but I needed to grow up, get out, and be responsible for myself. So that's exactly what I did. I moved on and began to live this thing called life.

Chapter Two

Fast forward to age thirty.

I was offered a great opportunity to work for a small, but stable law firm as a Legal Assistant in Miami, Florida and Miami became my permanent home. Finally! All of my hard work and dedication had paid off. No more mediocre jobs for me.

This is the year I also met and married my husband, Matthew. I'll never forget the day that I first laid eyes on him. We were both at a local event called Music in the Park. I remember that day so clearly. What drew me to him was his beautiful smile. I've always had a thing for men with a great smile.

I was waiting in line to purchase a cherry Slurpee. The humidity and heat was in full swing that day. As I was waiting in line, that's when I noticed him, Matthew. He was approaching the same line that I was in. We gave each other a smile, said hello, and introduced ourselves. As I was about to pay for my Slurpee, he nicely asked if he could pay for mine as well. I took him up on his offer. As he was handing the guy the money behind the counter, he turned and asked me if we could chat for a little bit. I agreed.

We walked around the park while still listening to the music in the distance. That's when we found out that we both had a passion for music. We talked about every genre that you can think about. Our connection was immediate. It didn't feel awkward at all. It was almost like we had been friends for years. The connection felt good to me and he made me feel comfortable.

We decided to take a break from the heat, so we found a little bit of shade by the fountains and sat down on a bench nearby. We talked about a lot of things: family, friends, our jobs, things we enjoy doing, and anything else that we could think of. I learned that Matthew is the eldest of three siblings and he comes from a tight-knit family. He worked for a large distribution company as a Warehouse Supervisor in Miami. His best friend James died in his sleep from natural causes a year before we met. Eventually, we lightened the conversation and began to discuss what we enjoyed doing in our spare time as well. I couldn't believe that we had so much in common.

As time went on, we discovered almost everything there was to know about each other. Matthew, I knew without a doubt, was comfortable with me because of how openly he discussed even the most personal aspects of his life. I didn't mind it at all. The connection was real, very real. This was all too good to be true. Have I met my soul mate? Could he be "the one?"

Four hours had passed by and Music in the Park was coming to an end. People started leaving and booths had begun to close. Matthew and I were still talking. I knew in my heart that this wouldn't be the last time we saw each other. I believe Matthew could tell that I was winding down as the night came to a close. But, before we parted ways, he asked me if we could see each other again and we exchanged phone numbers.

He proceeded to walk me to my car and, just as I unlocked my doors, he opened my car door for me. *What a gentleman.* I rolled down my window once I was in my car to say a final goodbye. Before I pulled off, he gave me a big smile and said, "We'll see each other sooner than you think." I looked down at my watch; it was 6:37 p.m.

As I drove off, I couldn't help but think about Matthew. Was he real? I mean, was he truly the real deal? When would he call? Would he even call at all? Is he involved with somebody else? I had a thousand questions racing through my mind. He was perfect. He was everything I could've ever wanted in a man. In those four

5

hours we spent talking to one another, I felt that I knew so much about him that I wanted to marry him. I know that's not the norm, thinking about marriage after knowing somebody for only four hours, but this was special. I knew it.

It was 8:30 p.m. when the phone rang. I answered, and it was Matthew on the line.

"Hello beautiful! Are you well rested after our long day?" he softly chuckled.

As I smiled, I answered, "I sure am. I needed the rest."

"So, are you doing anything tonight?" he asked.

"No, I'm just relaxing for the evening."

"That's too bad. I have a nice Italian restaurant in mind that I think you would love."

I paused for a bit. I was comfortable and relaxed, but what the heck.

"Okay, let's go for it!"

We discussed the time he'd be picking me up, I gave him my address, and got off the phone to get ready.

Matthew picked me up at 9:30 p.m. As we were driving off, he was going on and on about what a great restaurant we were going to. I couldn't wait to get there because I didn't each much that day. We had been driving for about fifteen minutes when I asked how much longer it would take to get there. He quickly glanced at me and said, "Right about now. We're here."

As he parked the car, I couldn't help but think to myself that he had good taste. He came around and opened my door and we went inside the restaurant. We were warmly greeted before being seated. The location of our table was in a great spot. We had a beautiful view of the water. The décor was absolutely stunning.

Matthew suggested some of the best dishes they served on the menu. After looking over the menu, I opted for the Stuffed Chicken Marsala. Matthew ordered the Lasagna for himself and Red wine for the both of us.

As we sat and enjoyed dinner, Matthew seemed a bit quieter than earlier in the day. I mean, we still had great conversation, but something felt different. Things got silent and he asked if he could ask me a question, a serious question.

He started off by saying that he'd never met a woman so special and he knew that he wanted me. The way he looked at me when he spoke made me want him. I wanted him lying next to me every night. But we just met. It was too crazy!

When he finished saying what he needed to say, I looked at him in a way that let him know I felt the same way too. I opened my mouth to reply, but instead he leaned over and kissed me on the forehead. I knew right then and there that this was the perfect man for me. He was handsome. He was respectful, kind, funny, and most importantly to me, he didn't have any kids of his own yet. I didn't have any children either, and this meant that we would have the chance to make a family of our own.

The restaurant was going be closing soon, so we finished up and he drove me back home. Although it was late, I invited him in for a slice of cake I had baked the previous day. I developed a love for homemade cakes from my mom and dad. They were always baking for their shop and I always watched them when I was a child.

Matthew was delighted when I asked him to come in. What I liked most about him was that although we both expressed how we felt at the restaurant, he was a "no pressure" kind of man. He didn't try anything funny that night. He was a gentleman. I respected him for that.

He stayed for about an hour and he seemed to be enjoying my lemon-coconut cake.

"Do you mind if I have another slice?"

"Of course. You can have as much as you want," I answered flirtatiously.

He looked at me and shook his head with a slight grin. After he finished up his second piece of cake, he got ready to make his way home.

"I had a great time tonight."

"Likewise. I really enjoyed your company," I responded with an uncontrollable smile on my face.

Before he left, he kissed me on the forehead and this time he kissed me on my nose, too. I thought that was so cute and giggled as he headed towards the door and out towards his car.

Twenty minutes later Matthew called me to say he had made it home safe and we said goodnight to one another. Before we got off the phone, I thanked him again for the wonderful evening and for being a gentleman. He told me it was his pleasure, and we hung up.

I woke up the next morning and glanced over at my alarm clock. It was 8:10 a.m. The first thing that came to my mind was the beautiful evening that I shared with Matthew the night prior. I laid there for about fifteen minutes reminiscing. I then got out of bed and freshened up. I wasn't too hungry, so I just made some green tea and grabbed one of my word puzzles. I've loved word puzzles since I was a little girl. My dad and I used to compete to see who could find the most words in ten minutes. About thirty minutes in to my word search, not to my surprise, the phone rang and it was Matthew.

"Good morning beautiful!"

"Well good morning to you too handsome! How did you sleep last night?"

"I slept just fine. But I woke up thinking about us. I was wondering if you'd like to come to my place so that I can show off some of my cooking skills. I was thinking about making us some brunch around noon."

"I would love that! Sounds like a plan to me."

"Perfect! I know exactly what I'm going to cook for you. Make sure you bring a big appetite with you!" he laughed. "So, I guess you'll need my address, won't you?"

I laughed and said, "I believe that's the way it works."

After Matthew gave me his address, we got off of the phone and told each other that we looked forward to seeing one another later on. I decided to put away my word puzzle and watch TV for a while.

After about two hours of watching TV, I decided to go in my closet to see what I was going to wear. I didn't want to overdo it, so I opted to wear my favorite pair of jeans, a teal top, and my brown strappy sandals. I applied very light makeup to my face. I normally liked to wear eyeliner, mascara, and lip gloss.

Noon finally came, so I grabbed my purse and made my way over to Matthew's house. As I was driving, I couldn't help but notice how well-kept the people's lawns were on his street, including his. I parked my car and went up to his door to ring the door bell. Matthew opened the door.

"Come on in!"

As I entered his home, the aroma of the food he was cooking smelled so delicious. He told me to make myself at home. Before I could sit down on the couch, he turned to me and gave me a warm hug. It felt so good to be in his arms. He then led me into his kitchen. I couldn't believe all of the food that he had cooked for just us two. I was impressed.

"Have a seat Ms. Hannah-Marie," he offered as he pulled out my chair for me.

"Why thank you. Everything looks so good. I must admit, I'm truly impressed."

Matthew winked at me as he turned to get the plates and silverware.

"You're in for a treat! I'm a great cook!"

"I can't wait to dive in."

"What can I start you out with?"

"Give me everything. I want to try it all."

Matthew had cooked us some omelets stuffed with spinach, mushrooms, cheddar cheese, yellow onions, and bell pepper. There was also some bacon and sausage for the side, AND pancakes made from scratch. He really out did himself. Did I mention that he made freshly squeezed orange juice, too? Yes he did.

As we were sitting at the table eating, Matthew started up a conversation.

"So, is everything to your liking?"

"Matthew, you've really out done yourself! Everything, and I mean EVERYTHING, is delicious!"

Matthew chuckled, "I told you I was a great cook!"

"You weren't lying about that. How did you learn how to cook like this?"

"My mom and dad are both great cooks. When I was in high school, I used to go in the kitchen and watch what they were doing. They enjoyed cooking together."

Matthew and I finished up our brunch and headed to his backyard where we continued to talk. We sat out there for about an hour before we came back into the house. He asked me if I wanted to stay a little longer and watch a movie, so I did.

As we were watching the movie, he gently placed his left hand on my thigh. *My goodness! How am I supposed to focus on the movie now?* He had such a gentle touch, but it sent chills up my spine. My mind was all over the place. I was no longer into the movie, but he didn't know that. I leaned in a little closer to him to let him know that it was okay.

"I want you in my life. I want you in my life to stay."

My heart started pounding because of what I had just revealed.

"Matthew, I can't believe I'm saying this, but I think you're the one."

Matthew let out a sigh of relief as he reached for my hand.

"Will you marry me Hannah-Marie? I know we've only known each other for a few days now, but I can't let you get away. I promise to show you unchanging love for as long as you let me."

Without any hesitation, I said yes.

Matthew hugged me as tight as he could and what came next really shocked me. He looked me in my eyes, rubbed his hand across my face and kissed me so passionately. His lips were so soft and his body felt so good against mine. I knew this was right. We kissed and felt all over each other and I could tell he was very excited, if you know what I mean. I liked what I felt in those jeans of his, and trust me, my body was responding too. The way he touched me made my body weak. I loved the fact that he was so gentle with me. He not only respected me, but he respected my body too. I could tell that, overall, he was a gentle natured man.

After things calmed down a bit, we just took some time to look in each other's eyes. Matthew looked at me with those sexy eyes and it was like I was under his control. *This man is truly something special, and he's mine,* I thought to myself. Matthew didn't want me to leave, but he remembered that I said I had an early morning, so we wrapped things up and he walked me out to my car. We said our goodbyes with one final kiss.

Mondays were extremely busy at the law firm, so I didn't normally look forward to them. But today, however, was a special Monday. I received a bouquet of white Lilies, light pink Roses, and a card that read "Thank you for saying yes! I can't wait to make you Mrs. Anderson." Everybody at my job kept coming over to my desk admiring the beautiful flowers that had been sent to me.

Later on that week, Matthew called me and asked if I was free that coming Friday night after work. He wanted us to take a quick road trip to visit his parents in Savannah, Georgia for the weekend. He went on to say that he had talked so much about me and his parents couldn't wait to meet me.

Friday after work, I came home, freshened up, and got packed for our trip. I was a bit nervous, but excited at

12

the same time. All kinds of thoughts raced through my mind. *Will they like me? Will they think that we're crazy for getting married this soon? Will they think I'm good enough for their son?*

The drive up there was beautiful. Matthew and I passed the time by listening to all of our favorite songs. He had a massive CD collection in his car. We also discussed when we were going to get married, the colors of the wedding, and how many children we both wanted. We agreed that two would be enough; preferably a boy and a girl.

We finally made it to his parents' house and my stomach was filled with butterflies as if I was a teenager all over again. After meeting his parents and his siblings, I was relieved. They were all so kind and welcoming. There was a lot of laughter the whole time and they didn't question us about marrying so soon. They gave us their blessings and welcomed me into the family. I must admit, I was shocked. No questions at all, just a day filled with fun and lots of great cooking. Matthew was telling the truth. His parents could really cook.

Later on that evening, we all sat around the fireplace drinking wine with a platter of cheeses, meats, crackers, and fresh fruit that his mother made for us. This was a pleasant trip indeed.

The following morning, we headed back home. I advised Matthew that I would like him to meet my family as well. The day we met at the park, I told him about the death of my parents, so he knew that he was going to be meeting my uncle and his family as opposed to my parents. The traffic wasn't bad on the way from his parents' house, so we decided we could go ahead and stop by my uncle's house on our way back to Florida.

My uncle wasn't expecting us, but I knew he would be okay with us stopping by. Matthew wasn't nervous at all. In fact, he was excited to meet my family. Again, we had a fabulous visit with my side of the family. Everything went well. My uncle looked at me, gave me a smile, and nodded his head. I knew he approved. He just wanted me to be happy.

Within that same month, Matthew bought my ring. I wanted a diamond wedding band, but he wasn't having that. He said that his wife was going to have the best, so he bought me a two karat diamond ring. He spoiled me like crazy. Every time I looked around, I was getting some kind of new gift from him.

Every weekend for the past month, we had been going out and about doing all sorts of fun things together: rollerblading, paddle boating, jet skiing, going to the amusement park, swimming, etc. I can't even begin to explain how much fun we had been having. We were truly meant for each other, and I enjoyed every bit of it.

Six months after we met each other's family, Matthew and I made the decision to start looking for a home together. It didn't make any sense to live in two separate places, especially when we were spending all of our time together and, of course, planning on getting married. We were both renting our current homes, so we were ready to take the next step and become home owners.

We ended up buying a cozy house with three bedrooms and two and a half bathrooms that was closer to Matthew's job. It was perfect for us and we couldn't wait to start our own family. It had a beautiful backyard that would be perfect for family get-togethers and our future kids. Our kitchen allotted ample of room for both of us to be cooking at the same time. The master bedroom was to die for, and the other bedrooms were good sizes as well. We couldn't have been happier. This was the start of our life together.

A year after meeting one another's parents, Matthew and I tied the knot. We had a small, intimate wedding with close friends and family in our backyard. The weather was perfect! Matthew and I both looked stunning on our special day. This would be a day that we would never forget.

His mom and dad did all of the cooking and my family did all of the decorations. We received an abundance of gifts and cards with money in them. My uncle gave us $1,000 towards our honeymoon. If I had to describe this day in one word, it would be blessed!

Our honeymoon was fabulous. Maui, Hawaii was our destination of choice. We had a blast! For three days and three nights, we created lasting memories for the both of us.

The first night there was the most memorable one by far. Matthew and I made love for the very first time. He didn't believe in sex before marriage, and I was okay with that. I couldn't help but respect a man that felt this way, especially in this day and time. Besides that, we didn't want to make sex the root of our marriage. We both wanted to make sure that this was real and not just a physical thing.

Having sex with Matthew was well worth the wait. I could tell by his strong and lasting erection that night that he was well overdue. The love that we made that night was magical to say the least. I know I did my job because Matthew blurted out, "You're all woman Hannah-Marie" as I was on top of him riding him slowly. We both left each other more than satisfied that night. It was a night filled with memorable, passionate love making.

Two years into our marriage, I started feeling sick to my stomach very frequently. I went to see my doctor and, just as I thought, I was pregnant. Matthew was SO excited! It was like he had won a million dollars. He couldn't calm down. He grabbed me and rubbed my stomach after I told him the great news.

"I'm going to be the best father ever!"

"I know you will be, honey!"

Eight weeks later, I knew that something wasn't right. I was spotting and had severe lower back pain. I went back to see my doctor and she delivered the bad news to me: I miscarried our baby. I couldn't believe this was happening. I went into shock. Then I felt guilty. *Was there something that I did wrong? Am I too old to carry a child? I know I'm only 32, but did I wait too late? Oh my God! Matthew's going to be devastated.* My mind was being pulled in every direction. I experienced every emotion imaginable that day.

Matthew was at work, so I couldn't build up enough courage to call and deliver the bad news to him. I just couldn't. I waited for him to get home and then I told him. He asked if I was okay, held me close, and broke down crying. It was rough for him. He wanted this baby so terribly bad. I was devastated too, but Matthew took it much harder than I did.

A year later we decided to give it another try. I was scared of what could've happened, but we both wanted kids, so NOT trying again wasn't an option.

The second time around was a success. I found out that I was pregnant with twins. One was a boy and the other, a girl. Matthew and I told both sides of our families and they were all excited about the news. Of course we named the boy Matthew Jr., but we went back and forth on the girl's name. We eventually agreed on the name Chantal.

At eight and a half months, the doctor had to deliver the babies by C-section. We had to stay in the hospital for four days, but the babies and I were okay. My doctor just wanted us to stay in the hospital because the twins came a little early. They needed to be monitored throughout the night just in case there were any sudden changes with their health.

After the babies and I came home, Matthew was so ecstatic to be a new father and knew I could use the help, so he took off of work for a month. I was on maternity leave for three months. Things actually went smoother than I thought. Matthew definitely did his part. Watching him feed the babies, change their diapers, and talk to them was simply warming to my heart. We both enjoyed bonding with our little ones.

It had been three weeks and I was getting kind of sad because Matthew was going back to work soon. He'd been so good with the twins. I couldn't believe it, but he was taking this on like a champ. He hadn't complained one time. He loved laying the babies on his chest. He'd always say, "Do you hear daddy's heartbeat?" He was so gentle with them. I enjoyed watching him as he put them to bed. A loving dad he was, that's for sure.

Matthew went back to work, so it was just me and the twins now. My uncle's wife and my cousins drove down to see the twins, but my uncle was sick with the stomach flu, so he couldn't make it. My in-laws as well as a couple of mutual friends drove down to visit the little ones. The twins were pretty much sleep the whole time as everybody took turns holding them. They were such well-mannered little bundles of joy already. They hadn't cried a lot, and they pretty much only woke up when they were hungry or needed to be changed. I kept my fingers crossed, but at that point, it was good.

Time was nearing for me to go back to work, so we decided to start our search for childcare. After looking around and interviewing people, we decided to go with this lady who had her own private daycare in her home.

She was well-known around our neighborhood and many people highly recommended her. She had taken care of many older kids in the community. Her name was Ms. Frankly. She was a very nice woman who was very soft spoken. Her home was nicely kept and we could tell that she was an orderly woman. Everything was in its place whenever we walked in. The smell of her home was airy and fresh. The babies seemed to be happy and content. This would be Matthew Jr. and Chantal's permanent daycare, and we were both at peace now. We knew Ms. Frankly would take very good care of our babies.

Matthew Jr. and Chantal had finally turned one year old, and they were still bundles of joy. They were walking, talking, and feeding themselves. Chantal seemed to be a little stronger than Matthew Jr., but he followed right along behind her. They played so well with one another and they already had their own little personalities. Chantal was a little bossy at times, while Matthew Jr. was a laid back little guy.

Work was still going great for the both of us. Our kids were healthy and happy, and our marriage was still going strong. Life was good and there was no stopping us.

Over the next ten years, our family would experience some unpleasant events. We found out that Matthew Jr. had asthma, and it was incredibly severe at times. Chantal had serious allergies in the spring, and it sometimes affected the way she breathed. My hours at work had been reduced to part time. And so much for growth at the law firm, we lost a huge account that we were banking on.

Matthew got laid off from his job. Their production was extremely slow, so they had to lay off 100 employees. And, to top things off, I had a scare with breast cancer but, thankfully, my results came back negative. For the first time in our marriage, we felt like our backs were up against the wall. Our love for one another was truly tested. We had some arguments, but nothing to really worry about. It was a challenging time for us, but we made it through together.

When Matthew had finally got back to working, things were just getting back to normal for us. I must admit, things were getting a bit strained. Matthew lucked up. He got hired at a company that was even closer to our home. I was still working part time, but I was also baking and selling cookies on the side.

Let's fast forward to senior year in high school for Matthew Jr. and Chantal.

As parents, we couldn't have been more proud of what these two young adults had become and accomplished. We couldn't believe that they were on their way to college. Matthew Jr. wanted to be an Electrical Engineer and Chantal wanted to be an Accountant. They both worked hard throughout the years and their hard work paid off. They were both awarded scholarships for their academic achievements. I wished that they were attending the same college, but it didn't work out that way. Matthew Jr. wanted to attend a college in Southern California and Chantal wanted to attend college in New York.

Now that the kids were out of the house, it was just Matthew and I. We both had a hard time adjusting to them being gone, but we had to realize that we raised two well-rounded young adults, and that they would be just fine. It was our time now.

I decided to do something special for my honey's 50th birthday. He loved to be out on the water, so I rented a boat for his special day. He absolutely loved it! I chose not to invite any of our friends or family because I felt that we needed this time alone. We needed to bring back what we used to have. We needed that spark. I was missing the old Matthew.

Matthew had been a wonderful father to our children, but somewhere in between, we lost us, our connection. We became so preoccupied with raising the kids and working that we forgot to nurture our relationship. Don't get me wrong, Matthew was still a wonderful man, but let's just say that he was lacking in the bedroom. Seriously lacking! He also wasn't that charming and romantic guy that I had first met. And not that it was a big deal, but he didn't surprise me with special gifts like he did earlier in our marriage. I know that we were older and established now, but in my eyes, that shouldn't have changed our love for one another.

I had many talks with Matthew expressing that we needed to bring back what we used to have. He always said that he didn't see anything wrong. He insisted that he hadn't changed. He was always quick to say, "I work hard for this family. My family means everything to me." My rebuttal was always, "Honey, I know you work hard and take care of the family, but I need more." These conversations eventually turned into arguments and we got nowhere.

Over the next five years, our marriage was very unpredictable and challenging. One minute things were like the old times, and the next, we'd be arguing over the smallest things. Matthew and I were best friends, so it was difficult for me to grasp how we got there.

Something was very wrong with our marriage, but I couldn't put my finger on it. The funny thing about it was that I never entertained the thought of Matthew cheating on me. It just wasn't in his character to do something like that. I knew that my husband loved me dearly, but what was bothering him?

At one point in our marriage, Matthew would come home late from work and he would look so drained. I would cook his favorite foods, but he would sometimes say that he wasn't hungry. I would ask him if he wanted

20

to listen to some of our favorite songs, and he would express that he'd had a long day and that he was extremely tired. We used to love to go on long walks together, but that slowly faded out as well.

One night I came to bed with one of his favorite night gowns I used to wear. It was a silk lavender gown that went down to my ankles. Although it was long, it showed off all of my curves that Matthew was crazy about.

"Hey baby! Do you see like what you see? I've got the lavender on tonight. Your favorite."

Matthew looked at me and gave me a faint smile.

"I'm sorry baby. Not tonight. I just feel so drained. I need my rest."

I didn't have the nerve to start an argument because he did look very tired.

I got in the bed with my back turned to him. I can't deny it. I was a little bit upset, but I knew he was indeed tired. He moved closer to me and kissed my back.

"I love you Hannah-Marie. Goodnight my love."

"Yeah, I love you too Matthew. I love you too."

I knew Matthew could hear the frustration in my voice. At this point, I wasn't trying to hide it. What the hell was going on? I didn't know how much more of this I could take. I started to feel lonely in my own home. I didn't feel like we were best friends anymore. We used to have the best communication, but nowadays, I find myself begging for him to open up to me.

There were three more days until our 25th anniversary. As Matthew was sitting at his desk doing some paper work, he looked at his personal calendar.

21

"Can you believe it Hannah-Marie? We will be celebrating our 25th anniversary in three more days! I know that I haven't been the best husband for some time now, but I want to make things up for you, for us. So, what would the love of my life like to do?"

Although I appreciated my husband making the effort, I decided to go easy on him. Matthew just didn't look like himself.

"Let's go and enjoy dinner at the restaurant you took me to when we first met and then catch a movie? There are some really good movies out right now. Then if you're up to it, we can go have dessert at Bethany's Bakery."

"Are you sure honey, that's all you want to do?"

"I'm sure. As long as we're together, that's all that matters to me."

"Well then, that settles it. Back to where it all began," he winked.

Today was the day. Matthew and I were about to celebrate our special day. As we were getting dressed, we cracked a few jokes with one another. We used to always do that. We also had the music playing in the background and Matthew seemed to be in good spirits.

Unfortunately our special day didn't turn out the way we planned. Matthew got sick at the restaurant. He couldn't hold his food down, so we went home. I don't know what happened. He was in good spirits and then boom, he gets sick all of a sudden. I asked him if everything was alright and he said he just needed some rest.

Not to sound insensitive, but *here we go again*, I thought. He needed rest. At that point, I couldn't help but to wonder what was REALLY going on, so I had to ask.

"Matthew, is there something you have to tell me?"

"What do you mean honey? I'm fine."

"I don't think you're being upfront with me, Matthew. Something isn't right. Tell me what's going on."

"I assure you Hannah, I'm fine. Trust me. Can you please get me some water?"

"Of course. But if you're keeping something from me that I need to know, you're going to get it."

I went to get Matthew his water, but when I came back in to the room, he was already half way asleep, so I just left it on his night stand. Matthew was the kind of person that could fall asleep immediately.

While he took a nap, I went into the living room to watch T.V. I was sitting there all alone, and that's when the thoughts started swirling in my head.

What if. What if I could make up the perfect man for me? It was clear to me that Matthew was no longer the perfect man for me. Not by a long shot.

All I knew was that I desired more than what I was getting from my husband. And that's when all of the memories of Christian, Liam, and Bryce began to flood my mind.

Chapter Three

I met Christian the day before my 21st birthday. I was at the grocery store on the ice cream isle trying to figure out what kind of ice cream I wanted to buy. It was kind of embarrassing because I was talking to myself out loud when suddenly I heard this voice answer back to me.

"I highly recommend Ben & Jerry's Cherry Garcia."

I turned around and my eyes grew bigger. There standing before me was a tall handsome man who smelled really good.

"Is that right?" I answered in a soft, sexy kind of voice.

"Yes! Cherry Garcia is my favorite hands down."

"Hmm, I normally like ice cream with a bunch of stuff in it like nuts, caramel, and chocolate. I like ice cream that's busy, if you will."

"Oh, I see. Well, let's see what they've got here."

He actually took the time to help me read the ice cream labels to find a match.

"I think I found something that you might like. The label says it has chocolate ice cream with brownies, fudge, pecans, and caramel. This sounds perfect for you."

"Wow! That does sound delicious. I think we've got a winner."

He reached into the freezer and got a quart from the back and handed it to me.

"By the way, my name is Christian."

"My name is Hannah-Marie. You're too kind! Thank you for your help."

"It's really no problem. My pleasure! So, are you going to eat that all by yourself?"

I laughed out loud.

"Well, to be honest, yes I could eat this all by myself, but it's for my birthday tomorrow. I'm turning the big 21."

"That's exciting! I turned 21 last year and I had a blast! My friends got me real good. They planned a surprise party and, surprisingly, they got it past me without throwing any hints. They did well. It was a birthday party that I'll never forget."

"Lucky you! I'm sure you won't."

"If you don't mind me asking, what are you doing for your birthday tomorrow?"

"It's going to be pretty low key. I'm just inviting a few friends over, nothing spectacular. I know I'm turning 21, but I don't really feel like clubbing or anything like that. I just want to have a good time eating, laughing, and doing karaoke with my girls."

"Okay. That sounds cool. Do you mind if we exchange phone numbers? I would love to get to know you better, if you're okay with that."

"Sure. I don't mind at all."

We exchanged phone numbers and wished one another a good day.

Finally, it was my 21st birthday and I was feeling and looking my best. My friends were going to be over in a little while and I couldn't wait to see them.

My phone rang and it was Christian. He called to wish me a happy birthday. We didn't stay on the phone very long because I was busy getting things together for my company later on. He told me to have a good time and that we would have to chat soon.

My birthday was a success. My friends and I had a fun time, and I received some pretty nice gifts too. I can't remember the last time I've laughed that much. It was perfect. There was a lot of laughter throughout the night, and that was exactly what I needed.

The next day I called Christian and told him about the party. He was happy to hear that I enjoyed my friends. A couple of his friends were throwing a party at the roller rink, and he asked if I wanted to go with him.

I ended up going to the roller rink. His friends were down-to-earth and friendly. As I was lacing up my skates, Christian kissed me on my cheek.

"Are you sure that you're going to be able to keep up with me woman?" He said with a laugh.

"Just watch me. You have no idea what you're working with. I've been known to tire people out. I've got some serious skills. The real question is: Will you be able to keep up with me?"

"Ooh, I see I've got a cocky one on my hands. I like that."

"Me cocky? Not at all. I'm just very confident. Now follow my lead and you just may learn something tonight. I hope you brought your A-game." I winked.

Christian chuckled, reached for my hand, and led me to the floor where we skated all night long. I must admit, he was pretty darn good on his skates. He could skate backwards just like me. And, when a song came on that we both liked, we really tried to show each other up.

It was all in fun though. Christian was very respectful, attentive, and charming. We all ended up having a pleasant evening.

Christian and I ended up dating each other for the next two years.

Whenever I was with him, he made me feel like I was the only girl in this world, literally. He was the kind of man that opened car doors, held the door open, and pulled my chair out for me whenever we would go out to eat. Christian was an excellent communicator, too. I really appreciated that about him. I received flowers from Christian every Friday. This is something that he took pleasure in doing. He would do it just because.

Even on my bad days, he would tell me how beautiful I was. I can honestly say that he always made me feel special. It just came naturally to him to treat me with importance. I loved the way he gave eye contact whenever we talked with one another. He wasn't the best in bed, but he was very romantic, and I liked that a lot.

When it came to showing his appreciation for me, Christian would give me a full body massage. He was good at using his hands. I liked the fact that I didn't have to ask him to do special things. He knew just what to do and when to do it. He was special like that.

The only thing that I wasn't fond of was his lack of commitment to keeping a job. In the two years that we dated, Christian went through five jobs. I could never understand why. He was a great person, but when it came to work, it was challenging for him.

Although he got an A+ in romance, I knew that one day I wanted to get married and have a family, so I couldn't ignore the fact that Christian couldn't keep a job.

It was a Thursday afternoon when I told Christian that we needed to talk. I expressed to him how I felt about the job situation and he completely understood. He didn't have an attitude or anything.

"I know, it's my fault. I just have a hard time putting up with my bosses. A lot of them are just controlling and like to throw their power around."

"Yeah, I guess that makes sense, but you're not going to like everything about your job."

"I know, but this is something that I'm very passionate about. Not liking something small like my hours is one thing, but being disrespected is another."

He stood firm on what he had to say, but even after we agreed to part ways, we promised to still keep in contact with one another. There were no hard feelings between us. He fully respected how I felt and thanked me for being open and honest with him. We gave each other one final hug that seemed to have lasted forever. He kissed me on the hand, and that was our last physical contact with one another.

Chapter Four

A year had gone by before I met Liam. Liam was every woman's dream when it came to looks and sex.

I met Liam one day when I was working out at the gym. He stood 6'3 and he had a body to die for. His body was on point from head to toe. You could tell that he took working out very seriously. He had the sexiest hazel eyes. His hair was dark brown and super curly. Did I mention what gorgeous skin he had? Simply breathtaking! The skin complexion on his body looked like water and oil had been rubbed all over him. His skin had a natural glow to it. That smile of his would melt any woman's heart. Boy oh boy, and those hands of his. Oh my goodness! He was a sexy one indeed.

He had the full package, and I wanted to know more about him, so I walked over to him and introduced myself while he was taking a break from doing arm curls.

"Hello. My name is Hannah-Marie. Are you a new member? This is my first time seeing you here."

He smiled at me and extended his hand.

"And my name is Liam. Yes, as a matter of fact I am new. I've only been working out here for about a week now. What about you?"

"Well, I try to work out at least four times a week, but sometimes my schedule won't allow it. I try my best though."

"Hey, something beats nothing. At least you're making an effort."

"Yeah, I guess you're right. I personally like to run on the treadmill, work on my abs, and keep my inner thighs tight."

"I like it all. I enjoy everything that has to do with working out. I've been athletic since high school, so it comes easy for me. I guess you can say that I'm a workout junkie."

"No complaints here. You look great, but I'm sure you get that all the time. You body is amazing!"

"Thank you. I try. So, if you don't mind me asking, do you normally workout at this time of the day?"

"Yes I do. I like to beat the late afternoon rush. If you come too late, it's hard to get the machines you want."

"I'm sure. Well, I don't mean to rush our conversation, but I don't want my muscles to get cold and tighten back up. Do you mind giving me your phone number?"

"No I don't mind, as long as you call."

"You can bet on that. I will be calling you. That's for sure."

"Sounds good. Well you better get back to doing what you were doing. I'm about to go work on my abs. Have a good workout!"

"You too Hannah-Marie. See ya later!"

As I walked away I switched my bottom a little harder than usual. I wanted him to see what I was working with. I didn't look back, but I knew he was looking. How could he not? The spandex against my ass was fitting pretty darn snug. I couldn't wait for him to call. He was so fine! I'd be pretending and fooling myself if I didn't admit to what went through my mind. Thoughts of him doing some things to me. Some things that I surely wouldn't mind.

A couple days later, I received a call from Liam.

"Hey you! What cha got going on today?"

"Well, I was thinking about hitting the pool. Do you swim?"

"Swim? Do you know what they used to call me back in high school? The fish! I love the water!"

"The fish?" I asked as I laughed hysterically. "You've gotta be kidding me!"

"Nope. That's what they used to call me, seriously. I was the fastest swimmer in the county. I have two gold medals to prove it."

"I believe you. Wow! That's awesome. What can't you do?"

"I'll tell you what I can't do: Miss out on going swimming with you today. So, where are we going swimming?"

"There's a huge pool three blocks away from my place. It's a private pool within a subdivision, but my friend gave me the code to enter."

"Cool! Do you want to meet there or do you feel comfortable with me picking you up."

"Well, to be honest, because I'm just three blocks away, you can drive to my house and we can just walk if you don't mind. It's not too hot today."

"Sure, that works for me."

Liam showed up, and I literally had to compose myself. Damn he was sexy! He had his shirt off, so I was able to see his chest up close and personal. Those thoughts entered my mind once again. I was visualizing what he would be like in bed. Call me a bad girl all you want to, but he was a rare breed. I wouldn't mind him having his way with me. That's for sure.

Liam and I stayed at the pool for four hours. There were some other cool people there, so we started a game of volleyball in the pool. Of course Liam just had to show off. But, I guess he couldn't help that he was good at everything. He taught me how to swim backwards without sinking to the bottom. I rode on his back as he walked through the deep parts of the water. After having a blast in the pool, we enjoyed some sun on the lounge chairs. That was a memorable and fun day!

A week later, Liam invited me over to his place for a family BBQ. His family was a bit, well, let's just say that they were a unique family. That's putting it nicely. They all seemed to be enjoying themselves to some degree, but there was a lot of drinking and then came the family arguing. Liam apologized for their behavior. I could tell that he was embarrassed, but I didn't allow that to ruin my mood. Liam was a great host and that's all that truly mattered to me. He was really cool and I was into him.

After the BBQ, I noticed that nobody else was offering to help, so I took it upon myself to pick up the weight. I stayed behind to help him clean up. He was grateful and thankful for my help.

After we cleaned up and got everything back in order, he thanked me again. This was the first time that I saw a softer side to Liam. That made him even more attractive to me. He asked if I wanted to stay and keep him company for a little while, but I lied and said that I had other plans. I knew if I stayed, we were bound to have sex that night. My hormones were all over the place, so I did what I felt was the right thing to do at that time.

However, two weeks later, Liam came over to my place because I had invited him over for dinner one evening. I cooked some of my favorites: roast beef, mashed potatoes, fresh spinach, and I baked a strawberry cake.

As Liam ate his dinner, I couldn't help but notice how neat he was with his plate. He didn't like his food to touch. It took me back in time for a minute. My dad was the same way. He didn't like his food to touch either.

"Hannah-Marie, you sure have outdone yourself. Everything is so delicious!"

"Why, thank you Liam. I'm glad you're enjoying it."

"Enjoying it is an understatement. You can really cook!"

"You're too kind. Thank you!"

After dinner, Liam and I decided to go on a short walk around my neighborhood to walk off the food and make room for dessert. It was an enjoyable walk. We talked about our past relationships. Some of the stories he told me were truly funny.

When we came back in from our walk, I asked Liam if he wanted to freshen up a bit. He took me up on the offer because he was pretty sweaty after the walk. I handed him some clean towels and pointed him to the shower. While Liam was in the shower, I couldn't help but wonder what he looked liked naked. I went back and forth in my mind. *Should I go in there? What if he's not even thinking like I am? Would I scare him away? What would he think of me? Am I moving too soon?*

I built up enough nerve right as he was coming out of the shower.

"I'm sorry Liam. I was actually just coming in to grab a hair tie to put my hair up."

Now mind you, Liam is standing there dripping wet looking as fine as ever. He didn't even flinch when I walked in. He just stood there rubbing himself dry. I took a quick glance between his legs, and that's when he replied.

"It's all good Hannah-Marie. I'm sure you've seen a naked man before. And plus, we're both grown-ups."

Feeling a bit nervous, I told Liam that I would let him finish up.

Now it was my turn to freshen up. By this time, I was in need of a cold shower after what I just witnessed between his muscular legs and thighs. I couldn't even think straight when Liam came out of the bathroom.

"All done! I believe it's your turn now. Boy did that shower feel good. Thank you for the offer."

"You're so very welcome. I won't be long. Just make yourself at home."

About three minutes into my shower, I hear a knock on the door.

"Come in."

"I apologize Hannah-Marie. Do you mind if I grab something to drink?"

"Oh, no problem Liam. I told you to make yourself at home. Really."

"I just wanted to make sure that I asked before I went into your refrigerator."

"Have at it."

Liam closed the door and left out. Damn! All I could think about was how I wished he would have walked in on me while I was just coming out of the shower.

After I finished up with my shower, I came out and Liam was flicking through the channels on the T.V.

"Hey! How was your shower?"

"Nice. Real nice! I have some movies underneath the T.V. if you want to look through them."

"Sure. That sounds good. It doesn't seem like there's much on T.V. right now."

Liam looked through most of my movies and he found one that he liked.

"What about this one?"

"Great pick. I can watch this one over and over. I love action packed movies. Are you ready for the cake?"

"I sure am. I'd like a big slice, please."

"Coming right up! I think I'm going to treat myself to a big slice too."

We watched the movie while we ate our cake. We ended up pausing the movie three times. We also ended up eating ¾ of the cake. I made it extra moist with extra strawberries.

Liam asked me if he could stay the night because it had gotten late and he didn't want to be out on the road. I told him that I didn't mind at all. He spent the night on my sofa bed. In the middle of the night, I peeked in the living room to check on him, and he was fast asleep.

The next morning he woke up at 5:30 a.m. He had to get an early start because he had promised his friend that he'd help him move. His friend lived an hour away, so he wanted to get an early start to miss any possible traffic. Before Liam left, I fixed him a cup of coffee and offered him a blueberry muffin. We hugged, slightly kissed, and he was on his way.

Three months later.

Liam's friend had a timeshare in New York City, New York and he offered it to us for free for two days and two nights. How could we pass this up? It was free! Liam wanted to fly, so he paid for our plane tickets.

I remembered that when we first touched down, I was in awe by all of the supersized buildings.

"Woo-hoo! I'm in New York!" I said with so much excitement in my voice.

"Yes you are! And I can't wait to show you a good time!"

Liam and I freshened up and changed our clothes before we hit the town. It was a little bit after lunch time, so we decided to grab a bite to eat first. We opted for seafood, and boy was it tasty! After that, we walked around taking in the beauty of the city. Later on that evening, Liam said he had a surprise for me. He had purchased some tickets for us to enjoy a musical that night. The tickets weren't the only surprise that I received that night. He bought me some fine chocolate, a dozen of white roses, and the cutest little bear.

Everything was amazing that night. The musical kept me captivated the whole time. The restaurant that Liam took me to had excellent grilled salmon. I was in heaven.

When we got back to our room for the night, Liam flopped down on the oversized king bed.

"What a night! Please tell me that you enjoyed your surprises."

"I totally enjoyed everything! It couldn't have been better."

"I'm so glad to hear you say that. I was hoping that you would."

"You did good Liam. You did good."

"Well, I don't know about you, but I'm going to take advantage of that luxury, jetted tub in there. Do you care to join me?"

"Are you sure?"

"Hannah-Marie, trust me. I'm VERY sure. We've had a long day. We deserve to unwind in style. Besides, it's not like you haven't seen me naked before."

I shook my head and laughed.

"Well, you do have a point. But you haven't seen me naked, now have you?"

"Well, it looks like I'm about to be a lucky man tonight. Seeing your body for the first time, that is."

I bent over to take off my heels and I heard Liam make some kind of noise underneath his breath. I continued to undress when Liam asked if he could help me unzip my dress from the back. As he was unzipping my dress, he moved closer to me and pressed his penis against my ass. I had a G-string on, so I could feel his soft skin against mine. He ever so gently pulled down my panties, and I knew what was about to take place. There was no way I was going to stop him. I had been waiting for this moment. I wanted him bad. I wanted to feel him inside of me and on top of me. I wanted to feel every inch of what he had to offer.

Liam turned me around towards him and he passionately kissed me. I had never been kissed like that before. He kissed with so much passion. When he started sucking on my nipples, I almost lost it. My vagina got so wet and I began to cream. He sucked on my nipples just right. Liam bent me over the jetted tub and licked my clitoris. He licked and sucked, then licked and sucked some more. Oh my goodness! I was so weak in the knees that I could hardly stand up.

"Liam. What are you trying to do to me?"

Liam didn't answer me. He kept on doing what he apparently wanted to do. Pleasing me. He then carried me over to our king sized bed.

"You know you've been wanting this Hannah-Marie. I've seen that look in your eyes."

Before I could answer him, he put his tongue down my throat and got on top of me. As he was kissing me, he looked me in my eyes and inserted his throbbing, thick penis in my sticky wet vagina.

"You like that, Hannah-Marie?"

I could barely get anything to come out. I was trying to relax every muscle in my body so that I could take in every inch that I had been longing for. I managed to get out two words.

"Yes, baby!"

Liam started off really slow because he could tell that I was super tight. I hadn't made love to anybody in over a year. Once it was in all the way, Liam really went to town. He fucked the hell out of me. He didn't have any mercy. He made sure that I felt all that he had to offer and then some. When he put me in the doggy style position, he went nuts. I quickly found out that this was his favorite position. Every now and then he would spank my ass and open my legs wider so that he could go deeper.

"Hannah-Marie, I'm about to cum baby!"

Liam took out his penis and squirted his cum all over my ass. The next thing that he did was so respectful and different. He went into the bathroom to get a warm, lightly soapy towel so that he could wipe the cum off of my ass and to wipe my vagina because it was sticky. After that, we took a nap because we were both tired. He held me close the whole time we slept.

We slept for about two hours and then got up. Liam looked over at me with a smile on his face.

"Guess what." Liam exclaimed.

"What?"

"I'm craving you again."

"You've gotta be kiddin' me."

"I'm serious. Touch it and tell me what you think."

I put my hands on Liam's penis and he was hard again. Brick hard. He took his fingers and started rubbing on my clitoris. The way he kissed me by my ear sent chills down my spine.

"Are you ready for round two?"

"I don't know, Liam. I'm still recovering from the first round."

"I'll be gentle baby. I'll go really slow. Is that okay with you?"

"Yeah baby. It's okay. Go slow though. You've got me sore."

"I promise baby. I'll take it easy."

Liam kept his promise. Slowly, he entered inside of me, but it still felt nice because his penis was not only thick, but long too. I loved the way he teased me by taking it all the way out, teasing me with the head, and then going all the way in. It amazed me how he was able to stay hard for so long. He took his time with me. At times, he would stop and kiss me all over. There was no rushing. We took our time and enjoyed every moment. He was perfect!

The next morning we woke up, he had ordered room service for us. We ate and hit the town for the last time. We didn't go all out because, to be honest, we just didn't have the strength to do anything extravagant. As a matter of fact, we called it in early at about 6:30 p.m.

As we were headed back home on our flight, we both just looked at each other and smiled. No words needed to be spoken. We both knew.

For the next year, Liam and I were still at it as if it was our first time making love with one another. Our sex life was more than satisfying. There was never a dull moment in the bedroom. We kept it fresh and new.

A year and nine months into our relationship, Liam was offered a job transfer that he couldn't turn down. This opportunity would take his career to a whole new level. I knew it wouldn't have been fair to try to stop him or make him feel guilty. His company paid for everything for him to move to their new office that would be located in Seattle, Washington.

We were both at peace. We understood that sometimes you have to do what you have to do. I mean, I completely understood. That's why I moved to Miami, Florida.

We kept in contact for the first year and a half, but eventually, we started new lives. We were too far away from one another, so we finally gave each other the go ahead, and we both moved on.

Chapter Five

I was picking up my dresses from the dry cleaners when I met Bryce. As he stood in back of me, I kept thinking to myself, whoever is standing behind me sure smells really good. I shifted my body so that I could get a peek out of the side of my eyes. When I saw what he looked like, I couldn't help but to look him up and down. As I turned back around, I couldn't believe I had just done that, but he was so handsome! He was a well put together man from head to toe. His suit looked like it was tailor-made. It fit him perfectly.

I was next in line to get my dresses. I reached in my purse to get my debit card, when the man behind me told the guy behind the counter to put it on his bill. I looked back.

"I hope you don't mind."

"Umm, I can't let you do that. I don't even know you, but thank you anyways."

"Please allow me to pay. It's just something that I enjoy doing."

"You mean to tell me that you go around just paying for people's stuff?"

"Well, not quite like that. Once a month I like to sporadically do a kind deed for somebody. No strings attached. Just being kind."

"Wow! How kind of you. That is quite nice indeed. I can respect that. Sure. Sure you can pay for my items. I appreciate it."

As he stepped in front of me to pay the bill, I took advantage of the opportunity to look him up and down once again. Handsome was an understatement.

Everything about this man was neat. Who was he? What was his name? I was going to make sure that I found out before I left.

"Excuse me. You didn't tell me your name. I'm Hannah-Marie, and you are?"

"Pardon me. My name is Bryce. Bryce Colton."

"Well, thanks again, Bryce. I greatly appreciate your kindness. You have a pleasant day."

"If you're not in a rush, I'd like to ask you a question before you leave. Just let me finish up paying here. Give me a second."

"Sure. I'm mean, how can I say no to somebody who just took care of my bill? I'll be waiting outside."

Bryce came outside and he walked over to his car. His car matched his choice of clothing: very stylish and classy. It was apparent that he had expensive taste.

"So, Hannah-Marie, are you available?"

"Available? What do you mean by that?"

"Are you single?"

"I most certainly am. Who wants to know?"

"Oh, I see you have a sense of humor. I like that."

"I'm sure you do. How is somebody as nice-looking as you single?"

"So what are you saying? A good-looking, professional man who has it all can't be single?"

"No."

Bryce started laughing really hard. A gut-wrenching laugh.

"You are just my type. You're a feisty one I see. One that speaks her mind. I love that!"

"I bet you tell all the women that. What do you really want from me? I thought there weren't any strings attached."

"I'm sorry if I'm making you uncomfortable. I'm just having fun with you. Seriously, no strings attached."

"I know you are. I'm just giving you a hard time is all."

"I would love to take you to breakfast one day. I know most men ask women out to dinner, but I know this fabulous breakfast café right by the beach. Everything is always fresh."

"I guess I'll give you a shot."

"You won't be sorry. We'll have a good time, and we'll definitely enjoy our food."

Bryce and I exchanged numbers and parted ways. Although I had his phone number too, I purposely didn't call him first. It actually took him a week to call me. He had to go out of town for several business meetings.

Two weeks after we first met, Bryce finally took me to have breakfast. The food was all that he said it would be. We had a nice time, but he couldn't stay long. He needed to finish up some important papers, but he swore that he would make things up to me.

The following week, Bryce called me and asked if I wanted to accompany him to his company party. He said it was formal dress attire and that the party was being held at the Palms Lille, which was a very upscale hotel. I agreed to go. I knew that I would have a good time. What was not to like about a venue like that?

Bryce and I had an okay time at his company party. I kind of saw a different side to Bryce that night. I don't want to sound too critical, but he definitely likes to be the center of attention. I didn't find that to be very attractive. He spent so much time mingling with other people that I began to question why I was even there.

Everybody seemed to be having a grand time. Bryce hadn't asked me to dance yet, so I took charge and asked him.

"Hey! Let's get out on the dance floor and show them what we've got."

"I'm going to have to pass on this one, Hannah-Marie. I'm not much of a dancer. Trust me. I can't dance to save my life."

"Oh come on! I'm sure that you're not that bad. What's a party without dancing? And plus the music is great! Come on."

"I can't. I'm not going to make a fool of myself. You go dance and I'll watch."

"I'd rather not. You invited me, so I would like to dance with my date. Oh well. Never mind."

After that, things were a bit strained, if you will. It just didn't seem to flow after that. We stayed for two more hours, but it felt weird. I couldn't believe he didn't like to dance. I'm not going to lie, at that moment I felt like I didn't know how it was going to work out between him and I. I love to go out dancing and I love good music.

Bryce continued to demand attention by making himself the center of attention. During some parts of the night, all I could do was shake my head in disbelief. When he wasn't busy parading around, he introduced me to just about all of his co-workers. Aside from Bryce being cocky and somewhat inconsiderate, the food, music, people, and venue were all memorable that night. I made the best of it. I just felt that Bryce was a bit stiff. He was a little on the conservative side to me, and I wanted to have fun. He fell short that night, and I wasn't planning on another date.

When Bryce and I left the party, he looked at me and could tell that I wasn't too thrilled about that evening.

"Hannah-Marie, did I do something wrong?"

"I could complain, but over the years I've learned that people are who they are. So with that being said, don't sweat it. I'll be okay."

"No really. What did I do? I would like to know."

"Are you serious, Bryce? You spent more time parading around than anything else. I didn't feel like you were a good date tonight. I was NOT impressed with your behavior. Not at all."

"Well I'm sorry that you felt that way. I was just being me."

"Exactly. That's why I said I'll be okay. In other words, don't worry about it."

"You know, I have an image to uphold. I try my best not to put my guards down too much. I like to still remain professional, even though we were at a party. It's still my job. I'm sure you can respect that."

"Of course I respect that. I just felt that you could have been more attentive. Let's just please let it go. It's been a long night, and it's late."

"I just don't want there to be any hard feelings between us."

"There won't be. Like I said, I'm okay."

The drive home was quiet. Neither one of us had anything to say after that. I think that we were both ready to go home and call it a night. I know for myself, I was beat. I needed some rest and I couldn't wait to get home.

To my surprise, Bryce called me the very next day. He apologized for making me feel left out and for not paying enough attention to me. He pleaded for another shot. He asked me if I liked to travel, and I told him yes. In three more weeks he was going out of town again and he wanted to know if I would like to fly down on the weekend of his stay. He assured me that it would just be him and I. He was going to allot the weekend for us to have some fun.

Bryce bought me a first class, round-trip ticket to Charlotte, North Carolina. He picked me up from the airport with a dozen of red, yellow, and white roses. What made it extra special was the smile that came across his face when he saw me.

"Welcome to North Carolina! How was your flight?"

"Everything went well. Thank you for asking. Wow! What lovely roses. Thank you! You're starting off good, I see."

"This weekend is all about Hannah-Marie. I've got some making up to do."

That same day, Bryce planned a picnic in the park for us. Everything was to my liking. Later on that evening, we took a stroll in the park, and that was nice as well. The conversation was flowing and things felt nice. After that, we grabbed a bite to eat at a deli nearby. We sat outside of the deli, ate, and talked some more. Bryce asked me if it was too late for ice cream and I told him it was never too late for ice cream. After we finished up our sundaes, we headed back to his hotel room.

We got up early the next morning, went on an early morning jog, and then ordered room service for breakfast. Later on in the day, we rented some bikes and went on a three mile bike ride. All I could think to myself was *wow! What a difference. He really does know how to relax and have fun.* I was truly enjoying that weekend and I didn't want it to end.

The following day would be my last evening in Charlotte, so Bryce made reservations at this upper class restaurant that boasted the best steaks, lobster, and crab in town. He wanted us to match for dinner, so we both wore gray and purple. As always, he looked incredibly handsome.

After dinner we came back to the room to dress down in comfortable clothes and then we took a late night walk.

"I can't thank you enough for your hospitality, Bryce.

"It was my pleasure. I told you this weekend was all about you, and I meant that. I can breathe easy now. You seem to be happy."

"Indeed I am. Thank you so much. It was so nice to see a more down-to-earth side of you."

Bryce laughed.

"I'm so glad you gave me a second chance. Again, I apologize."

"No worries. I really enjoyed myself tonight!"

As I was on the plane flying back home, I smiled at the real Bryce that I had gotten to know and replayed all of the fun moments that we shared in my head.

I saw a lot of different places that I had never seen before because of Bryce. His job involved a lot of time away from home, but he would always send for me wherever he was. Money wasn't an issue for him. He made plenty of it.

Bryce flew me out to New Jersey, California, New York, Arizona, Chicago, Pennsylvania, and many other places. It seemed like I stayed in the air. I was literally flying somewhere new at least once a month. Although I enjoyed myself with Bryce on these trips, it kind of grew old after a while. There I was thinking about the future again. I knew that I didn't want a husband who had to travel and be gone from home a lot. On top of that, I liked Bryce and what he had to offer, but I still felt like something was missing.

I enjoyed the perks, but we just didn't have a true connection. I was old enough to know that if something is real, you won't have to try to force it. We had fun. We traveled a lot. We ate at the finest restaurants, shopped at the most expensive stores, but that wasn't what I wanted for my life. I wanted to one day have a family man, and I knew deep in my heart that Bryce wasn't the one. I respected his dedication to his work, and I respected him being so driven, but it just wasn't for me. It was fun while it lasted.

I waited for Bryce to come home from one of his trips. I felt it was only fair that I come clean to him.

"Thank you for meeting with me. What I have to say may come as a shock to you, but I have to be honest with you. This just isn't going to work for me. Don't get me wrong. I know you have to travel a lot because of your job, but I want a family one day, and I want a husband that's going to be home with me and the kids."

"Hannah-Marie, I wish that I could say that I'm shocked, but I'm not. You see, I always run into this

49

problem with women. They love it at first, but then it gets old. I get it. I truly do. But my work comes first. I've worked too hard to let it go."

"I wouldn't dare ask you to change anything. I respect your hard work, I really do! I just know that down the line, I wouldn't be okay with this, so that's why I think it's best if we stop seeing each other. It won't make any sense to keep carrying on when we both know how I feel about all of the traveling."

"Can we at least stay friends?"

"I don't mind staying friends, but I won't be a traveling friend. I just think it's best if we cut ties on that level."

"No pressure. I just want to remain friends if that's okay with you."

"I'm okay with that."

Bryce and I are still friends to this day, but I never traveled with him again. I didn't want to fool myself into thinking things would change, and I was right. He's still traveling A LOT. He has yet to find a woman who can handle the extensive traveling he has to do. I personally believe that Bryce is, and always will be, married to his work.

Final Chapter

After days of entertaining the memories of my past relationships, I finally snapped back into reality. I realized that I still had a husband, and we had some things that needed to be worked out.

As I was in the kitchen cooking dinner, I heard keys in the front door. It was Matthew. He was home from work much earlier than usual. I heard him put his things down in the front room before he entered into the kitchen.

"Hello honey. How was your day?" he sounded a bit strained.

"It was good, Matthew. How was yours? You're home early."

Matthew slowly came over to me and I knew that he could hear the worry in my voice.

"That's what I wanted to talk to you about darling. I came home early because I have something important that I need to share with you. I can't keep doing this to you. You don't deserve this."

My heart started pounding rapidly. What was Matthew about to tell me?

"I don't deserve what? Matthew, please, what is it?"

"Honey, I think it'll be best if you finish up in here and then we can sit down and talk about this. It's going to take some time."

"I'm basically done. I just need to put the lasagna in the oven. Give me a second."

Matthew slowly walked over to sit at the table and waited for me to finish up.

"Okay. I'm done. What did you have to tell me?"

"I love you so much Hannah-Marie and I don't want to lose you. I haven't been honest with you. I've been keeping this secret for the past two years and it's time that I tell you what's been going on with me. It's affecting our marriage and I don't want you to think it has anything to do with you."

"Matthew, you're really scaring me. What is it?"

"I suffer from Erectile Dysfunction. I've been secretly seeing a counselor for the last year and a half for depression. I'm on anti-depressants as well. The medication that I take makes me tired and nauseous sometimes. I know you think that I don't want to make love to you because I've been pushing you away and telling you that I'm tired, but I was too embarrassed to talk to you about all of this."

"Matthew..."

"No, please let me just get everything out. I need to get this off of my chest."

"Okay honey, But-"

Matthew cut me off and continued to talk.

"I feel so guilty for keeping this from you. You are my best friend. I had no right. No right at all. I feel like I've been selfish. At the time, I didn't even consider how you would feel. I made this all about me, as if I would be the only one affected by this. I've never kept secrets from you. But I just didn't feel like a man anymore once I found out. I played with thoughts in my head that maybe you'd leave me. I don't know what I'd do if you ever left

52

me. I love you and our kids. You all mean the world to me."

"Matthew, I'm so sorry that you felt this way. I can't believe that you've been going through this alone. I'm sorry if I made you feel like you couldn't open up to me. You're right. We are best friends, and you should've felt more than comfortable to open up to me about this. I apologize."

"Hannah-Marie, this is NOT your fault. Please don't blame yourself."

"You've always been able to share anything with me and, for some reason, you didn't this time."

"Hannah-Marie, I won't allow you to carry this weight. Listen. I've been emotionally distant from you, and that's not fair. I have physically withdrawn from you and that's not right either. I've neglected you to a point where I know you've been feeling lonely and, for that, I feel horrible."

"Matthew, I love you dearly and you know that. No matter what, I'm here for you. I could stand here and point fingers at you and be angry, but I'm not going to do that. That's not what you or I need right now. We need each other. We will get through this together."

"I'm so sorry that I kept you in the dark. I had no right to do that. I've been dealing with anxiety, depression, and low self-esteem because of all of this. This has really been weighing on me. Keeping these secrets from you nearly destroyed me. And I can tell from the look in your eyes sometimes that you are growing weary."

"Yes. As a matter of fact, you're right. I was going down that path in my mind. But I have my answer now. I feel better that I know the reasons behind your actions. I thought it was me. I was beginning to feel like our marriage was over. I was wondering why you haven't been doing the things that you normally do to me or with me. Now I know."

As Matthew and I hugged each other, tears started to roll down my face. I felt horrible on the inside in regards to the thoughts that I had been having about Christian, Liam, and Bryce. For the past two years my husband has been feeling like he wasn't man enough for me, attending counseling, and taking anti-depressants. And to think, here I was thinking about my past relationships. *For as long as we've been married, why didn't I push the envelope and make Matthew open up to me sooner?* I knew something was wrong, but I just didn't know what at the time. I wish I would have pressed the issue. Maybe we wouldn't be going through this right now.

I could feel Matthew holding me tighter and tighter. The more I cried, the more he embraced me. I laid my head on his chest and allowed my body to fully relax against his. In that exact moment, I felt the genuine love between us. We were both vulnerable and we didn't care. This was clearly the old us. The two people that fell in love with each other many, many, many years ago.

Matthew wiped my tears with his favorite handkerchief that I had bought him a while back. He looked me in my eyes with such care, compassion, and love.

"Hannah-Marie, you are my heart. I knew that when I married you, you were something special."

I broke down crying once again. I know how much I mean to Matthew, and the thought of me entertaining those thoughts about my past relationships was eating away at me. Although they were just thoughts, I felt it was only fair that I told him about it. I pulled myself together and told Matthew that I needed to share something with him.

"What is it sweetheart?"

"I want us to have a clean slate. You came clean with me, so I want to come clean with you. I didn't actually cheat on you, but I have been thinking about some of my previous relationships. I've been wishing in my head that I could make up the perfect man for me."

Matthew held his head down for a moment and let out a sigh.

"It hurts to hear this Hannah-Marie, but how can I blame you? I openly admitted that I have neglected you. I haven't been giving you the love that you deserve. But, I'm willing to move forward and put all of this behind us. Are you?"

"You're not angry?"

"No, I'm not. I know my wife. I love my wife. I respect my wife. You're feeling like any other woman would feel. Lonely. And I'm sorry that I made you feel this way. You know that I would never intentionally do anything to hurt you. I adore you!"

"I know you do, Matthew. I adore you too. I'm one lucky woman to have married a man like you. I don't know what I was thinking. No man could ever compare to you. No man."

Matthew smiled at me with his beautiful smile, and I smiled right back at him. We sat down and discussed the details of his condition in more detail. He told me that he's going to try another medication to help with what he's going through. He's going to make an appointment with his doctor to be slowly taken off of the anti-depressants as well. He wants to continue with his counseling, and I agreed to attend some sessions with him for extra support.

I took Matthew by the hand and led him into our bedroom. I told him to sit on the bed while I looked in the closet for one of our wedding boxes where I kept our personal wedding vows that we wrote for each other. I read my vows out loud to him.

"My dearest Matthew, you are truly something special. You have such a big and loving heart. You have been patient with me in every way possible. You've been by my side every step of the way without any complaints. You are patient, loving, respectful, and most favorable of all, you are my best friend. I vow this day to always be there right by your side. I'll forever lift you up, never down you. I'll love you for who you are as a person. I'll always hear you when you speak. I'll be faithful. I truly value what we have. You are my soul mate. You give me complete happiness. I will be there in sickness and in health. If you fall, I'll be right there to catch you because you're that important to me. I love and greatly appreciate you."

Matthew broke down into tears after I finished reading the vows that I wrote for him 25 years ago and gestured for me to come lie in his arms.

"We were truly meant to be. We belong together, and we will stay together and weather any storm that may come against us."

"I wouldn't have it any other way, my love."

Matthew and I lied down on the bed and held each other close. As I laid there, thoughts raced through my mind again. No, not thoughts about Christian, Liam, or Bryce, but thoughts about my marriage.

I thought about how sometimes people can be going through some challenging times in their marriage, and they can allow their mind to wander. And, if you're not careful, you can ruin the best thing that has ever happened to you. I almost did that. Although they were just thoughts, I still allowed myself to entertain those thoughts. What if I had been a little weaker and acted upon them? What then? Would I still have my marriage? Could it have been saved?

Marriage takes a lot of work, commitment, and dedication. The question is, are you willing to fight for what's worth fighting for, and is your marriage important to you? Sometimes in life we can make horrible mistakes that we wish we could take back, but we can't. The damage has been done.

I learned a valuable lesson. Make sure that you communicate at all times. A lack of communication can lead to many things that will eventually end up hurting the one that you love and care about. When you love somebody, don't be so easy to give up. I'm not talking about if you're in just any old relationship; I'm talking about if you have a mate that's everything to you and then some.

I'm talking about somebody who makes you feel extra special. Somebody who loves, appreciates, and values you. Somebody who just simply adores you. Somebody who has your best interest at heart. I'm talking about THAT kind of love. Nobody, and I mean nobody, else would be worth losing that kind of love. This kind of love is genuine and rare.

So, with that being said, I'm grateful for this wake up call. After 25 years of marriage, I'm reminded all over again of the jewel that I have. Not four. Not three. Not two, but ONE man is the perfect man for me. And his name is Matthew.

Matthew and I value our marriage, and we're going to stick by each other's side through any obstacles that we may face together. We are in love with each other. We love each other as individuals, and we are one. We are love. At the end of the day, WE are all we've got. We started this journey a long time ago and there's no stopping us now. We both know what we have in each other and that's more than enough.

Marriage is not always going to be pretty, but Matthew and I are willing to paint a new picture. We're willing to paint a picture that represents what our marriage is really about, and that consists of love, courage, strength, and determination. Matthew was the perfect man for me then, and he's the perfect man for me now. No other man could ever compare to Matthew.

I have accepted where I allowed my mind to wander, because it just reminded me of what kind of husband that I have. Matthew has always been a wonderful father to our kids. He's always respected me as his wife, mother, and as an individual. He helps with cooking, cleaning, and he's always been a hard worker for this family. He has always made his family a priority, and I fully respect him for that. Matthew has supported me in whatever I've set out to do. I know without a doubt that he has my back. He's given me the kind of love that most women only dream of having.

I've questioned myself as to why I didn't look at the full picture from the beginning of me feeling the way that I did, but I'm thankful and grateful that I did not make any foolish mistakes that I would have regretted for the rest of my life. It's a good thing to stop, think, and play the tape all of the way through.

I've got the perfect man for me, and he's standing here right by my side.

A Note to My Readers

I would like to take this time to thank you for purchasing *The Perfect Man for Me*. I value my fans and readers. I hope that you enjoyed reading this short story as much as I enjoyed writing it. The best part for me was coming up with the names for my characters and bringing them to life. It was a lot of fun allowing my creative juices to flow.

I ask that if you enjoyed reading this short story, please let me know by writing an honest review on Amazon. I would greatly appreciate your thoughts.

Again, thank you, and best wishes to you!

www.ingramcontent.com/pod-product-compliance
Lightning Source LLC
Chambersburg PA
CBHW070353130626
46556CB00007B/3156